Map of
HIGH PARK
in
TORONTO

400 ACRES

Warabé

NESTING AREA

NATURE

TOBOGGANING

WEST ROAD

PICNIC AREA   PATIO

COLBORN LODGE DRIVE

NATURE TRAIL

ALLOTMENT GARDENS

T.T.C. LOOP

NATURE TRAIL

PLAYGROUND

PICNIC AREA

CONCESSION

WASHROOM

PICNIC AREA

TENNIS COURTS
ICE RINK

PARKING LOT

HIGH PARK SCHOOL FOR OUTDOOR EDUCATION

DISCARD

PARKING LOT

HIGH PARK FOREST SCHOOL
FOR VISUAL-IMPAIRED CHILDREN

PICNIC AREA

NATURE TRAIL

PICNIC AREA

PICNIC AREA

E.D. LOTT MEMORIAL

PLAYGROUND

HIGH PARK

MAIN

SUBWAY & BUS

BLOOR STREET WEST

KEEL SUBWAY & BUS

Who Goes to the Park

WARABÉ ASKA

 Tundra Books

When the ice melts on the pond,
Geese return to the park.
They make their nests and hatch their young
For the wind to cradle in gentle waves.
Let them teach the goslings to walk in water.
Little geese, little geese,
Soft as the springtime you are!

When the trees begin to sprout leaves,
Blackbirds appear in the park,
The great oak raises its arms
To hold all their songs in harmony.
Let us sing together a welcome to spring.
Great oak, great oak,
What a vigorous choirmaster you are!

When the spring sun grows warmer,
Whole families come to the park.
Children roll all over the lawn,
While grown-ups watch from the benches.
Let them play on the carpet of new grass.
Lively children, lively children,
How wonderfully carefree you are!

When yew bushes grow out of bounds
Schoolchildren come to the park.
As gardeners trim shrubs into shape
Small heads look at themselves in the pool.
Let us cut our hair too, before summer.
Boys and girls, boys and girls,
How very lightheaded you'll be!

When waterfowl swim two by two,
Young couples come to the park.
As swans signal love to each other,
The water reflects as a blessing.
Let us stand and hold hands as we watch.
New lovers, young lovers,
How gentle in love you all are!

When June flowers burst into bloom,
Wedding parties come to the park.
While doves coo their message of love,
Cameras picture a day to remember.
Let us smile on their time to be happy.
Brides and grooms, brides and grooms,
How beautiful love makes you all!

When the sun of summer turns hot
Mothers bring their babies to the park.
As the butterflies flit through the flowers,
They lend wings to our dreams for our children.
Let them carry our hopes to the sky.
Little angels, little angels,
What an infinite joy you are!

When the sky turns suddenly dark,
Stormclouds come over the park.
The thunder god bangs on his drums
And the band marches off as it answers.
Let us listen for who plays the louder.
Thunder, lightning, rain and wind,
What mean old spoilsports you are!

When Indian summer arrives,
Older folk come to the park
To bowl on the long stretch of lawn
In the lengthening shadows of fall.
Let us call to each other as we play,
Old friends, dear friends,
What pleasures and memories we share!

When the geese leave for the South
Sadness comes over the park.
Leaves blow like flags of farewell,
And doors shut tight against the cold.
Let us wish all the birds a safe journey.
Return geese, remember geese,
This is your home!

When the cold clouds pass over at night,
The trees stand alone in the park.
The moon sees them bend in the wind
As their branches, like children, hold hands.
Let us join their wild dance in the dark.
Lean trees, lonely trees,
What dancers in the wind you are!

When the first snow falls in the park,
The popcorn-man comes with his cart.
Sounds of Christmas ring in the air;
Children's hearts leap up to the sky.
Let us watch for the coming of reindeer.
Dear Santa, dear Santa,
How good we all suddenly are!

When water freezes over the pond,
Families of skaters come to the park.
As they blow their breath into the cold
Lilies of smoke float up and away.
Let us skate to trumpets of music.
Boys and girls, moms and dads,
How young together we feel!

When winter dresses all in fresh white,
Young hearts take over the park.
They throw fresh snow in the air
And like magic, snow geese appear.
Let us joy in the beauty around us.
All of us, all of us,
How happy we are in the park!

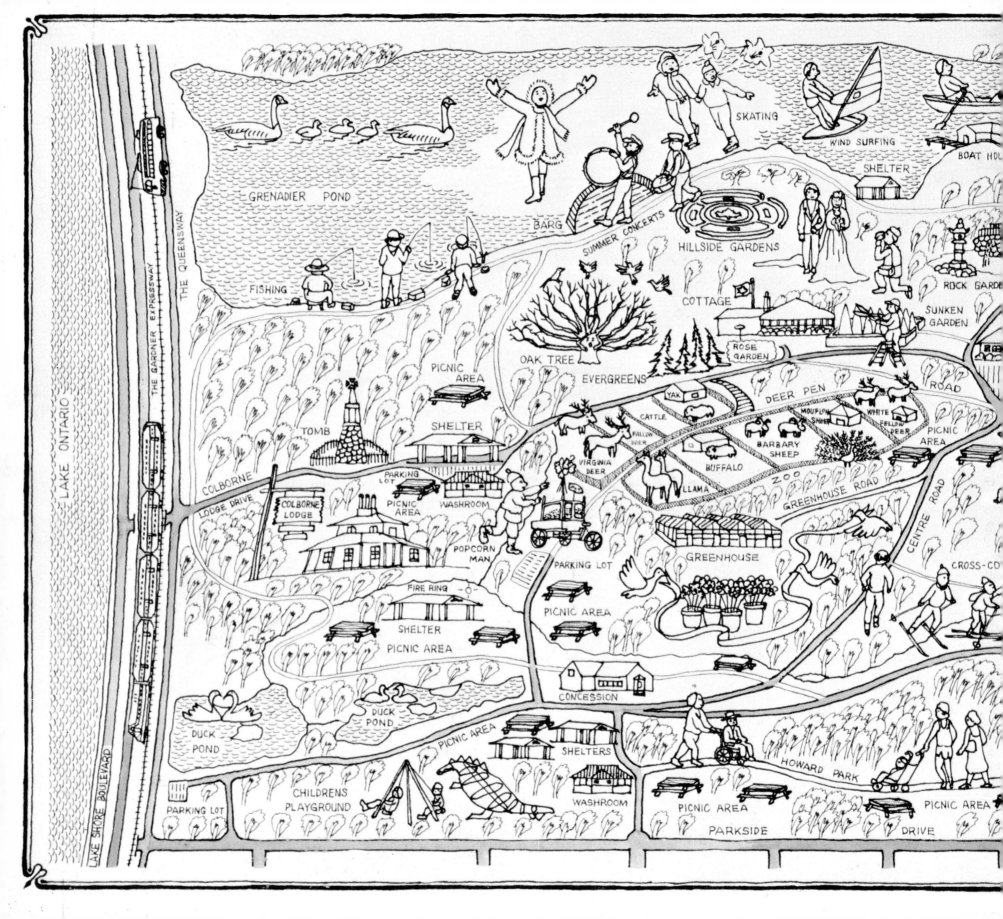